WEIRD
SPORTS
MOMENTS

By K.C. Kelley

The Child's World®

Published by The Child's World®
1980 Lookout Drive
Mankato, MN 56003-1705
800-599-READ
www.childsworld.com

The Child's World®: Mary Berendes, Publishing Director
The Design Lab: Design and production

Copyright © 2011 by The Child's World®
All rights reserved. No part of this book may be reproduced or
utilized in any form or by any means without written permission
from the publisher.

Photo credits
Cover: AP/Wide World: top and bottom right; Getty Images:
bottom left
Interior: AP/Wide World: 5, 6, 10, 14, 17, 18, 22; Getty
Images: 9, 13, 21.

Library of Congress Cataloging-in-Publication Data
 Kelley, K. C.
  Weird sports moments / by K. C. Kelley.
    p. cm.
  Includes bibliographical references and index.
  ISBN 978-1-60954-377-8 (library bound: alk. paper)
 1. Sports—Juvenile literature. 2. Curiosities and wonders—
Juvenile literature. I. Title.
  GV705.4.K45 2011
  796—dc22   2010042899

Printed in the United States of America
Mankato, Minnesota
December, 2010
PA02070

Above: The end of the weirdest play in football history. Find out more on page 10.

For more information about the photo on page 1, turn to page 22.

TABLE OF CONTENTS

Find out why this confused mascot held up an NBA game on page 20.

Sports Lowlights

We all watch sports waiting for a great moment. We look for the winning home run or the diving touchdown catch. After such plays, we talk about them with friends. "Did you see that? That was amazing!" The world of sports is full of such moments. This book is packed with the *weirdest* moments in sports. Not every play has a happy ending. Not every game is perfectly played. The stories in this book are just as real as a winning goal . . . just not as memorable for the athletes! Check out these sports "lowlights!"

Oops! These Cincinnati Reds players will probably end up on the blooper reel!

BONUS WEIRDNESS

We hope you don't think we're just making fun of athletes here. They're all doing their best. Just remember, nobody's perfect . . . and sometimes that's funny.

5

BONUS WEIRDNESS

Roy Riegels of California was the first famous wrong-way runner. In the 1920 Rose Bowl, he picked up a fumble and ran 65 yards the other way. He was tackled—by his teammate—just before the other end zone. It led to a safety for Georgia Tech, who won the game 8–7.

Great play! Marshall recovers the fumble.
Not so great play: He ran the wrong way!

The Other Way! Run the Other Way!

Jim Marshall of the Minnesota Vikings was one of the NFL's toughest defensive linemen. He just wasn't so good with directions. In a 1964 game, the Vikings were playing the San Francisco 49ers. The 49ers **fumbled** the ball and Marshall snatched it up. He started running for the end zone. It was a lineman's dream come true! One problem: He ran the wrong way! He sprinted 66 yards into his own end zone! He threw the ball into the stands, giving the 49ers a two-point **safety**. The Vikings won the game, but Marshall's run earned a place in the hall of shame!

Check Your Rear-View Mirror

Leon Lett taught us a lesson in Super Bowl XXVII: Don't celebrate too early. The Dallas Cowboys lineman was near the end zone after a long fumble return. He held the ball out to his side to celebrate. That's when Buffalo wide receiver Don Beebe caught Lett and whacked the ball out of his hand! No score for Dallas and Buffalo got the ball back! The Cowboys won the game 52–17, so Lett was off the hook.

Beebe (82) smacked the ball out of Lett's hands while Lett was looking back to celebrate!

BONUS
WEIRDNESS

Look, up in the sky! It's a . . . Viking? Before Super Bowl II, the Minnesota Vikings **mascot** was trying to land a hot-air balloon on the field. He was a better mascot than a pilot, however. The balloon crashed and collapsed! No one was hurt, but it sure was weird!

9

BONUS WEIRDNESS

Some odd touchdown celebrations from recent NFL seasons:
- Joe Horn of the Saints pulled a cell phone from his sock and pretended to make a call.
- Terrell Owens of the Cowboys took some popcorn from a fan and ate it!
- Chad Ochocino of the Bengals pretended to putt the football like a golf ball!

California's Kevin Moen is about the land in the end zone—and on the band!

The Band Is on the Field!

This is often called the wildest play in college football history. In a 1982 game, Stanford took the lead over California with four seconds left. Stanford then kicked off to Cal. Cal decided to pass the ball back and forth as they ran down the field. As Cal ran toward the end zone, the Stanford band thought the game was over . . . and it ran onto the field! Cal players had to dodge trumpets and drums as they returned the ball. Finally, Cal's Kevin Moen crossed into the end zone . . . smashed into a trombone player . . . and scored! A moment later, the refs said the bizarre play was good, and "The Play" entered sports legend.

Using His Head

Jose Canseco hit 462 home runs in his 17-year career. He used a bat for all of those. He also hit one with his head . . . and made history. In a 1993 game, Canseco was playing right field for the Texas Rangers. Carlos Martinez of the Cleveland Indians hit a long fly ball toward right field. Canseco went back . . . and back . . . but the ball bounced off his head and went over the outfield fence! It was a home run for Martinez . . . and years of laughs for Canseco! Some people call this the most famous blooper in baseball history.

The ball is on its way over the fence after bouncing off Canseco's head.

Here's another story about baseball and heads. Before a 1997 game, the Florida Marlins mascot, Billy the Marlin, was supposed to parachute onto the field. On the way down, his giant foam head fell off! It ended up on a nearby road. The mascot/parachutist landed safely (and headless) outside the ballpark.

In a 1981 game, Seattle Mariners third baseman Lenny Randle tried a new way to get a bunt to roll foul. He crawled after the ball and blew on it! The trick didn't work, but it has become a famous baseball blooper!

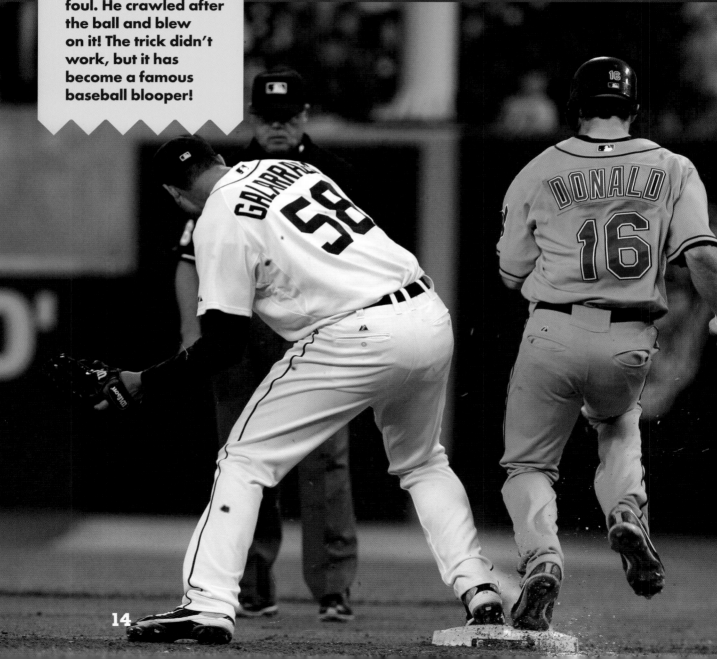

The ball and Galarraga's foot beat the runner to the base . . . but the umpire disagreed!

Close to Perfect

In 2010, Detroit Tigers pitcher Armando Galarraga was just one out away from a **perfect game**. He had retired 26 straight Cleveland Indians. The 27th batter grounded a ball toward first base. Miguel Cabrera fielded the ball. He threw to Galarraga covering first base. The pitcher's foot hit the base before the runner's. But umpire Jim Joyce called the runner safe! It was a terrible call, and even Joyce said so later. But the damage was done. No perfect game, not even a no-hitter. After the game, Galarraga was a "perfect" example of sportsmanship. He said it was part of the game and he had no hard feelings.

Crazy Night at the Ballpark

In the 1970s, a type of music called disco was popular with many people. It was also very unpopular with others. In 1977, the Chicago White Sox decided to get fans to come to a game by burning disco records between games of a **doubleheader**. They figured it would be a silly event for people who didn't like disco. They figured wrong. As the bonfire started in the outfield, fans rushed the field! They danced and ran around and ruined the grass! The White Sox had to **forfeit** the second game!

The disco haters stormed the field . . . and cost their hometown team the game!

BONUS WEIRDNESS

Baseball fans love to collect stuff from their heroes, but this was ridiculous. In 2002, a fan paid $10,000 for a hunk of gum chewed by Arizona outfielder Luis Gonzalez. Ewww!

BONUS WEIRDNESS

Football is not the only game affected by fog. In 2006, an ice hockey game between Boston College and Boston University had to end early. Why? A thick fog hovered over the ice and the players couldn't see the puck!

Somewhere in the fog, the Bears are about to snap the ball ....we think!

Can Anyone See the Football?

The Chicago Bears were leading the Philadelphia Eagles 17–6. It was the second quarter of a 1988 NFL **playoff** game. Things were going fine . . . until the fog rolled in. The Bears play in a stadium right next to Lake Michigan. Cool weather created a huge, thick fog cloud that covered the field. Fans in the stands could not see the players. The players could barely see each other. TV announcers could only stare at the fog and guess what was happening. The game went on! Each team struggled with the poor conditions, and the Bears ended up winning "The Fog Bowl."

More Than Just a Mascot

Before a 2009 NBA playoff game, the Atlanta Hawks released their mascot, Spirit, to excite the crowd. The trained hawk did more than that. Instead of returning to its trainer, Spirit had a little adventure. As players ducked away, the hawk swooped around the court. It finally landed on the clock above one of the baskets. The trainer eventually got Spirit to come down, but it delayed the start of the game. Maybe Spirit just wanted a bird's-eye view!

Spirit the Hawk held up the game when it landed on the clock above the basket.

How strong are NBA players? So strong that they can smash backboards and pull down nets! Shaquille O'Neal did it twice in 1993. One of those times he pulled the entire backboard to the ground! Darryl Dawkins twice smashed the backboard glass with shattering slam dunks! Look out below!

BONUS WEIRDNESS

Goalies in hockey sometimes score, too. The first was Billy Smith of the Islanders in 1979. The most recent was Miko Noronen of the Sabres in 2004. They all shot the pucks into empty nets after the opposing goalie was pulled late in their games.

This is how Luis Martinez must have celebrated when he scored an amazing goal!

Goooooaalie!

Goalies in soccer make very long kicks. They can kick the ball nearly the length of the field. In 2006, goalie Luis Martinez of Colombia boomed a kick from near his own goal. The ball flew down the field, high above the other players. It bounced in front of the other goalie, Tomasz Kuszczak of Poland . . . and then right into the goal! The crowd screamed! Martinez's teammates surrounded him in joy! And poor Kuszczak had to get the ball from the back of the net.

Glossary

doubleheader—two baseball games played on the same day by the same two teams

forfeit—to lose a game as punishment for breaking a rule rather than by the score

fumbled—dropped the football

mascot—a costumed character who represents a sports team

perfect game—a baseball game in which the pitcher does not allow a single baserunner by the opposing team

playoff—a game to determine a champion

safety—in football, a two-point score earned by tackling the opponent in his own end zone

Web Sites

For links to learn more about weird sports: **childsworld.com/links**

Note to Parents, Teachers, and Librarians: We routinely verify our Web links to make sure they are safe and active sites. So encourage your readers to check them out!

Index